WRITING BECKETT'S LETTERS

GEORGE CRAIG

Writing Beckett's Letters

The Cahiers Series

CENTER FOR WRITERS & TRANSLATORS
THE AMERICAN UNIVERSITY OF PARIS

—

SYLPH EDITIONS

Preface

SOME FIFTEEN YEARS AGO I WAS ASKED by the editors of *The Letters of Samuel Beckett* (then only a project, although based on the express wish of Beckett himself) to act as translator from French to English. I was coming to the end of an academic career teaching French, and was delighted at the chance to put such skills as I had in the service of a writer for whom I had boundless admiration. It happened also that I was Irish, and familiar with Beckett's world, above all with the paths by which his linguistic idiom, in both English and French, had evolved. No one should make such a claim unless he or she recognises that acquaintance, however detailed, brings no certainties – except one: that anyone offering certainties about language in general or translation in particular is either knave or fool. On the strength (or, as Beckett would probably have said, the weakness) of this conviction, I set to.

All except the crassest or boldest of translators live in the shadow of '*traduttore, traditore*' ('translator, traitor'). The only thing that can ease the discomfort and the guilt is the excitement of actually translating: setting up a body of words which, for better or worse, can stand for the original – and close the circle of engagement. For of course most translating is of complete works. No such comfort, however temporary, for the translator of Samuel Beckett's letters. Always behind the translator's shoulder is the man who could so easily and to such effect write his own letters in his own, native English. Worse, the letters are not a finished work, its overall shape settled by Beckett himself. On the contrary, they are the record of his arguments with himself (and others) about what such a work might be; and the arguments change with time. For the translator, quite simply, the task is impossible; and that is in fact a liberation. There is no ideal from which one's attempt

5

is a falling away, no discoverable way of doing it better. What follows here is an assemblage of links: to this moment or that, this memory or that, this bearing or that. All have their origin in words of Beckett's. The map they create is of the unpredictable variety of tone and preoccupation to be found in the letters. 'Correspondence', as Beckett practises it, is less the carrying out of a known task than a continual discovering of what in fact he wants to say, and how best (or, as he might put it, least badly) to say it.

George Craig, 2011

SAMUEL BECKETT

Paris
22.10.82

Cher Claude
Merci pour l'émouvante carte
fauteuil.
Très heureux de vous avoir revu.
En vous guidant j'avais Georges
à mes côtés.
Merci de me proposer votre
"commando". Pas question hélas.
Bien amicalement de
nous deux.
Sam

Between 1948 and 1952 there took place a particularly remarkable correspondence: that between Samuel Beckett and Georges Duthuit. In the course of his life Beckett wrote something approaching 20,000 letters. Fascinating as many of these are, they offer nothing that can match this explosion of words. But then Duthuit was not just any correspondent: he was a highly cultured and intellectually rigorous art historian and critic, with total confidence in his own judgement. For Beckett, recognising these qualities and drawn by Duthuit's impatient refusal of cultural orthodoxies, he represented something close to an ideal interlocutor: someone to whom, in the areas that mattered, *anything* could be said.

These voluminous letters are in French. Beckett's years in France – at first in Paris before the War, then, during the Occupation, in hiding in the South, finally, after the Liberation, back in Paris – were a time during which, slowly at first but with increasing urgency, the move to writing in French took shape. The risks were huge, but by the mid-1940s the impulsion was irresistible. It issued in two bodies of writing: the early stories and *Molloy*; and the letters. Duthuit, aware of Beckett's deep love of painting, wanted him to write about the artists whom they admired. Beckett, always uneasy when asked to produce formal criticism, wrote to make clear his ambivalence: the fears and the enthusiasm. He needed to believe that Duthuit could receive all this, and answer in kind. Small wonder that, when the signs were that Duthuit was indeed that kind of interlocutor, Beckett came close to idealising him: '*j'ai d'autres amis mais un seul Georges Duthuit. Je le sens. Je le sais*'. ('I have other friends, but only one Georges Duthuit. I feel it. I know it.') Within the freedom that this allowed, he wrote huge swathes of excited and extraordinary prose. With the confidence that this brought, his ability to follow the other promptings, to write on the *other* blank page (the stories, the novels, later the plays) grew more and more assured.

Like all idealisations, it eventually failed. For reasons that are unlikely ever to be wholly clear, Duthuit drifted away from Beckett. But the essential had been achieved. Beckett had established himself as a French writer.

'IL ÉTAIT EXALTÉ'

Thus Beckett's publisher Jérôme Lindon in discussion with me, when reacting to the prose of the letters to Duthuit ('He was overexcited'). But more is at issue than mood or degree of excitability, for here Beckett is urgently engaged in first-hand discovery of what he wants to say on a question of incomparable importance to him. A crude version of the question Beckett is wrestling with might be: how can I best explain to this powerful and sensitive art critic (Georges Duthuit) why Bram van Velde and Jack B. Yeats matter more to me than the other painters whose work I admire? Every attempt he makes sets up new difficulties, new possibilities of misunderstanding. No worked-out response predates this letter, these letters; the work is being done *in the letter(s)*. But Beckett is the first to see the dangerous implications of this emphasis or that, and is in there with the correcting pen before any emphasis has had time to harden into a statement or claim.

THE LETTER AND THE TEXT

One of the most prominent elements of those televised costume dramas so popular with British viewers is the preoccupation with the detail of life 'below stairs': the careful setting out of hierarchy and function. There may be chaos in the kitchen, but no hint of this or any other irregularity must appear in the servants' direct dealings with employers and guests. Discretion, to the point of near-invisibility, is what is required. Anyone editing or translating Beckett's letters would be ideally qualified for a part in one of these dramas. What must appear on the literary equivalent of the dining table or silver salver is an offering both appropriate and instantly usable: in this case, a clean and easily readable text (and where required its translation). This is something very remote from the origin of that text: the actual documents written (by hand or on his typewriter) by Beckett himself.

It is not in the fixities of print that we shall see Beckett in action – turning to this person or that, in this or that mood or degree of readiness – but in the surges of words, the crossings-out or underlinings, the marginal additions and postscripts. The letter

Ussy
20 juillet

cher vieux

is a physical reality: a visible record of what happened when he acted on the prompting to write to someone. Almost always, it is written rapidly, often in bursts, with pauses between the bursts. And 'rapidly' means, in practical terms, 'without reference to legibility'. Beckett is the first to recognise how difficult his hand is ('my Ogham'), and the letters abound in promises to be more careful, to do better. But these are like New Year resolutions: well intended, but never binding. The only exception (and without it we would not have had any letters, since they would never have reached the intended recipient) is the address: there we will see a fine clear hand – and sizeable lettering.

As translator, seeking to come as close as I can to the movements of thought and feeling, I am often faced with a scurry of strokes, some barely rising above a straight line, at the moments of greatest intensity. Needing most to be sure of my ground, I am confronted by opaque matter, in which it is not even certain where one word begins and another ends – or, just as important, which language these 'words' are in. In the worst case – excited letters to a very close friend who, for one reason or another, has had to move away – even the attempt to be legible disappears. The reaction that follows will be familiar to lovers of cryptic crosswords, as an obstinately asserted reading forms a prison ('it has to be that, yet it can't be that'). We may not be recognising the language in which the passage is written (Beckett never signals change of language, and such change is extremely common); or we may have been undone by his writing one word in two blocks, where for example there is a bulky consonant. (The reverse is also possible, of course: one apparent word for two intended ones.)

Short of publishing the letters as written, and converting every reader willy-nilly into an editor, there exists no good option but to issue a clear text. Yet the reader is less generously treated by this policy than the term 'clear text' might suggest. Beckett, that inveterate answerer of letters, only occasionally *wanted* to write to someone, and even then there was usually a practical justification for it. Once, and once only, in all the letters I have read have I found an unprompted beginning, when he says to Georges Duthuit, '*J'ai envie de vous écrire. C'est ma seule excuse*'. ('I feel like writing to you. That is my only excuse.') This greater or lesser distaste, the waxing or waning of each particular experience of distaste, can be glimpsed in the manuscript letters – in variations of spacing, of speed (with its inevitable effect on legibility), of length; afterthoughts, changes of tone, discontinuities – and is the visible representation of what Eliot called 'the intolerable wrestle / With words and meanings'.

Once in a while, in one of Beckett's letters – particularly in those to Georges Duthuit – something turns up that is not so much difficult as impossible: something offering no hint of how it might be resolved, or even understood. In its simplest form, first. Beckett is no great admirer of the novelist Raymond Queneau. Duthuit has suggested that Beckett might include something translated from Queneau by Beckett in an anthology he is preparing. Beckett says first '*Est-ce absolument nécessaire?*', and then quotes a few words: '*La servante, qui s'était* [*illegible word*] *dans la cuisine . . .*', about which he writes 'Translation: Who had wanted . . .' I can think of no French word that could both represent the illegible word and carry the meaning 'wanted'. The construction with '*s'était*' narrows drastically the range of possibilities; what follows must be a past participle, but no participle of the verbs of wanting (*vouloir, désirer, avoir envie*) could fit this syntactic frame. Nor could those participles which *would* fit, such as '*enfuie*', give any sense of wanting. Where to turn?

Beckett has no love for the Apostle Paul ('*ce salaud de Paul*' – 'that bastard Paul'), but grants that, at moments, his writing can almost match that of the Prophet Isaiah, whom he does admire. To Duthuit he quotes a long passage that ends 'There is a natural body and a spiritual body'. Then he adds, '*Autre chose quand même qu'Albert Bayet et Pierre Bénard*' ('A bit different all the same from AB and PB'). Undistinguished translators of the Bible into French, perhaps, a two-man team? In fact, Bayet was a sociologist at the Sorbonne, who occasionally wrote on religious topics. Bénard was the editor of the satirical and anti-clerical weekly *Le Canard Enchaîné*. What can have put these two in Beckett's mind, as representing presumably everything that the King James Bible was not? Why should he link the two men?

And we all know where you're not supposed to do that. First
check: has this really happened, or am I giving in to a prompting
from somewhere else, perhaps just a temporary preoccupation
of my own? Second check: what difference would my changing
the translation make, to the particular word or phrase, or to the
letter more generally? The commonest direction of change is that
of greater clarity, the most obvious kind of service to the reader.
But the text being considered is, for its own reasons, unclear, even
opaque. Novelists are not expositors. Where do letters stand, in
this perspective? Clarity may be an unquestioned good in business
letters, or in letters to someone hardly known. Between intimates,
no such norms apply.

'AUDITIF'

Beckett's letters to Georges Duthuit abound in strange,
unexpected things, but there can be few stranger and more
unexpected than the moment when he announces: '*Curieux
combien on est acculé au mot "écouter", nous qui ne sommes tout de
même pas des auditifs.*' ('Odd how often we are driven back on the
word "listening", we who are after all not ear-people.') No one
can read Beckett's novels or stories without being made aware of
the play of voice, of speech rhythms, of breath groups. This is the
man for whom every syllable in every play mattered: who, through
rehearsal after rehearsal, attended to delivery, to voice quality,
to vocal range. We are made aware in the letters of his delight
at having found the actors Jack McGowran and Patrick Magee,
to whom he could hand over his work without hesitation, in the
certainty that they could produce the sound-patterns he wanted.

But Duthuit is not just any recipient. There is the fact that
he is French: the letters form part of Beckett's first major
correspondence in French, and it takes place in the period where
Beckett's urge to make French his literary language is growing
in force. And then he is an extremely active and opinionated
art critic, who can spot a talent. The talent he spots is Beckett's
extraordinary awareness of – and familiarity with – European

painting, and he tempts (even *lures*) Beckett into writing about it. The inevitably visual aspect of this, coupled with the excitement and pleasure that Duthuit's encouragement has given him, surely prompt this apparent shift of perceptual allegiance. It will not recur.

It is April 1954. I am in Paris. I have just read *Malone meurt* (the second novel in the sequence *Molloy, Malone meurt, L'Innommable*). I am overwhelmed and yet, mysteriously, elated by it. At first, I don't know what to make of this. I have been asked round for a drink by a woman with strong literary interests. I tell her about what I've been reading, the overwhelmedness and the elation. She says that it sounds very strange, and asks where the elation could have come from. Suddenly I see, and the words come tumbling out. Beckett has invented a name (Saposcat), and this name fills me with delight. I *know*, in some peculiar yet commanding sense of that word, that this is a triumph for Beckett: that he has lovingly mouthed this alien construct – these consonants, these vowels, in this order – and quietly lodged it in the public domain, where no French reader will query it. This name (with its diminutive, Sapo) can stand for his whole (outsider's) enterprise: creating in the space of French.

A year earlier, just before I left Trinity College, Dublin, for France, my tutor handed me a note: a letter of introduction to his old friend Samuel Beckett. I was too timid to take up the opportunity. But I did make his acquaintance – in the terrain he might have preferred: written words.

'ÉCRIRE SUR' ('WRITING ABOUT')

Few words can produce a quicker reaction from Beckett than 'critic'. But what is at issue is much more than his dislike or distrust of professional commentators, well documented though that is. The phrase above, from a letter to Georges Duthuit,

mon cher vieux Georges

Bien content d'avoir [...]
tes nouvelles. Dix, ça c[...]
pas l'air potichon. M. Po[...]
ça a dû t'achever. U[...]
comme pourrissoir, on ne [...]
pas mieux. on s'y déco[...]
bien gentiment. en fais[...]
du rêve. Quel dommage [...]
s'ait choppé les policiers, [...]
n'en aurais fait qu'une b[...]
J'ai dégoté un abonneme[...]
lecture à La Terté, tu vo[...]
de tout repos, 15 francs pa[...]
somme pour 15 jours. J[...]
pris un livre sur Flau[...]
des lettres furieuses à Ma[...]
du camp qui m'ont réclam[...]
le coeur. mais quelle pun[...]
après le procès de Bovary [...]
que le connaisir, son écl[...]
l'impersonnel. mais en l[...]
tout pardonner à celui qu[...]
fait la fin de l'éducati[...]
ses appréciations littéraires, [...]
Je ne suis pas grand [...]
[...]devons. Quand il ne [...]
[...]voulera plus que s'aspir[...]
[...]au voyage. La semaine pro[...]

Cher vieux Georges

La glace est tou
traîtres, répartis
parents), Antenora
(traîtres des hôtes

Tu pourrais peut

O sovra tut
che stai ne
me' fóste

En fait de ver
qui puisse faire l'

Encore si les
mangeaient leurs pe

Poscia, più

Interpretatio
je tiens.

A bientôt, c

          mardi

au fond, au 9me cercle, réservé aux
tre 4 zones: Caïna (traîtres des
raîtres de la patrie), Giudecca
et Giudecca (traîtres des bienfaiteurs).

tre te servir des vers suivants:

e mal creata plebe,
luogo onde parlare à duro,
ate qui pecore o zebe!

          (32. 13-15)

descriptifs glacéés je n'ai rien trouvé
faire.

xxxxixxxxx de temps en temps les Innuit
ts, comme Ugolin...

e il dolore, potè il digiuno.

d'ailleurs fort douteuse, mais à laquelle

r vieux.

is the final, astonishing part of a refusal to write an appreciation of Bram van Velde that Duthuit has asked him to write. It runs: *'Je ne peux plus écrire de façon suivie sur Bram ni sur n'importe quoi. Je ne peux pas écrire* sur'. ('I am no longer capable of writing in any sustained way about Bram or about anything. I am no longer capable of writing *about.*')

If we could take that as a literal confession of limitedness ('I used to be able to do this kind of thing, but I can't any more', or 'I tried doing it, but I see now that it's no good just trying'), we could perhaps pass on from it without further comment; rather as if he had said 'I find my German isn't up to it any more'. But what is being said here, even when we allow for the qualifying 'in any sustained way', amounts to 'I can't do criticism'. That too is perfectly possible and untroubling in theory: why should he not keep away from the business of criticism, as he shies away from discussions of contract or promotional activities? But that is not what the letters tell us. In these we find judgements in plenty, short and long, favourable and unfavourable, often delivered with total confidence, sometimes hedged about with disclaimers, but always clear and careful. Accounts of what might be wrong with a performance are a particularly rich example, as are his occasional responses to younger writers' requests for reaction or guidance. Very occasionally his response to this or that is dauntingly abstract and extended, and we might start to wonder if after all we have got it all wrong. Then, a letter or two later, a correspondent asks if he has read this or that critic or philosopher. Beckett backs away at once: either he hasn't read him or he has tried and been defeated. Even Maurice Blanchot, one of the very few critics of whom he speaks with real approval, will lose him by being, in Beckett's view, too theoretical.

What sense can we make of these apparent contradictions? It might be better not to think of 'making sense of them' (with the implicit claim that we can see farther and straighter than Beckett), and recognise instead that they are simply (or complicatedly) indications that Beckett, in his own long search for what it is he wants to say, instinctively and properly backs away from any fixed position.

Moments when thought goes this way and that, pauses, restarts, and fails. Towards the end of one of his huge letters to Georges Duthuit, Beckett, over in Ireland to be with his dying mother, writes: '*Je guette les yeux de ma mère, jamais si bleus, si stupéfaits, si déchirants d'enfance sans issue, celle de la vieillesse*' ('I keep watching my mother's eyes, never so blue, so stupefied, so heartrending, eyes of an endless childhood, that of old age'). Heartrending indeed, but posing no great problem for the translator. Then a sentence later the original letter reads: '*Je crois que ce sont les premiers yeux que je voie. Je ne tiens pas à en voir d'autres*'. 'I think they are the first eyes that I....' That I what? The temptation is to go for 'have seen', leaving the reader free to add an explanatory note: 'the first he has ever properly looked at', or something of the sort. But he could have written '*que j'aie jamais vus*', which would mean precisely 'have seen'. And then, the verb is indeed '*voir*', not '*regarder*'. He can't possibly be saying that he has never seen eyes before, can he? Or expect us to supply the 'real' meaning: 'looked at'? And all this leaves out what the words actually say: '*que je voie*' – first-person singular of the present *subjunctive*. So we can't even rescue ourselves by a temptingly brilliant adjustment: 'the *earliest* eyes', for that would be a matter of historical fact, requiring only an indicative, '*que je vois*'. I am driven back on 'that I am seeing', but silently adding 'properly'. We all know what territory he is in; but not where he is standing. I have run out of track.

Anticipating what lies ahead for himself and Duthuit, Beckett continues, to his friend: '*Moi, je sais mal combattre. On fera peut-être quelque chose en ne pouvant combattre. Après tout c'est un talent répandu, celui-là. Dans la mêlée, bien sûr, pas au-dessus, poilu peu poilu indifférent aux causes.*' ('I am no good at fighting. Perhaps we can do something by not being able to fight. After all, that is a widely shared talent. In the free-for-all, of course, "*poilu peu poilu*", not above it, indifferent to causes.') The word '*poilu*' in standard French means 'hairy', and '*peu*' in this collocation means 'not very', but '*poilu*' in 1914-18 slang means 'soldier of low status', 'private' (someone from what the British army refers to as 'Other Ranks'). Somehow I must suggest this self-mockery in military terms, and so I take up the secondary meaning of 'rank' (foul-smelling, offensive) to go with the primary (ranker: man *in the ranks*). So, finally: 'rankest of rankers'. Well, yes, but...

PAR AVION

If there were an opposite of 'hype', what would it be? Exactly what is needed here: a way of pointing at a quirk of Beckett's: his continual scanning of descriptions of human behaviour (particularly his own) for signs of flattery, or indeed of anything complimentary, and the replacement of these by correspondingly unfavourable descriptions. All writers search, one supposes, especially since Flaubert and his insistence on 'le mot juste', for the 'right word'. Beckett in his last published text ends: 'What is the word'. For him, there could never be a *right* word.

A letter to a friend gives news of Beckett's progress: it is beginning to look as if a particular literary venture is almost complete. The expectable French would be that it was '*en bonne voie*'; for Beckett it was '*en mauvaise voie*'. Translating, I have to bypass 'well on the way' and move to 'ill on the way': the secondary meaning ('sick on the journey') reinforcing the refusal of confidence.

Reaching for a representation of himself and his French, Beckett focuses on '*un fort des Halles*' (a strapping, brass-lunged, 'alpha male' butcher's boy from the stalls of Les Halles) and comes up with this exhortation to himself: '*coule français de faible des Halles*' as the best he can hope to produce. English has no direct match – Smithfield does not seem to have generated a comparable popular mythology – and I find myself retreating to mere paraphrase: 'flow freely, weedy French' – what a '*faible des Halles*', if there were such a creature, would offer.

Beckett suggests to his publisher Jérôme Lindon that *Mercier et Camier* might, if Lindon is really determined to publish it, be included in a volume to be called *Merdes posthumes*. (He has just said that he would not want this piece to come out '*de mon simili-vivant*' – 'in my imitation lifetime', on the model of the French '*simili-cuir*', 'imitation leather'.)

Setting out, enthusiastically and energetically, on some project, Beckett finally has, as he puts it, 'the bit between his false teeth'.

Any English or Irish person over 50 is likely to have been taught at school by someone more (often much more) than five years older, who will have been taught by someone . . . and so on back to at least the time of Matthew Arnold. But usage changes over time. Beckett was born 25 years before me, his teachers proportionately before that; and he lived through two World Wars, against my one. Beckett's language is the set of his words for those experiences: the long continuities of academic discourse, the irruptions of strange new elements in wartime, and the continual recourse to other languages. Approaching Beckett's letters in my 70s, I have to ask, first, to what extent the set of my words overlaps with his. In the late 1940s, Beckett is still writing 'to-day' and 'to-morrow', still as often as not preferring 'they do not' to 'they don't'. How soon, if at all, will he adopt the more recent forms? 'If at all' is important: one may not only not take up a new usage; one may actively dislike it. These questions reappear whenever anyone sets about translating Beckett into English, and response will continue to change over time.

NO RESTING PLACE

If you can't be sure of the text that you propose to translate: confident, that is, that the words you are looking at (and by implication the alphabetical symbols with which they are formed) are indeed those written by the author, your prospects are not good. What is required is a mixture of luck, patience, memory, and openness; what is to be avoided is rivalry.

And supposing that I do eventually see what is being said – this word, these words in this sequence – how far on am I? Not much farther than when I am reading words that are not in doubt. For now I am facing a difficulty of a quite different kind: an invented word, an idiosyncratic usage, word-play. This time, unlike the relation between illegibility and importance, the difficulty may occur in what is usually seen as no more than elementary social requirements framing the letter proper: names, addresses, styles of greeting. A letter to Georges Duthuit opens:

Mon cher vieux Georges
Assez de ce vous garou, veux-tu?

At the time, the choice between '*vous*' and '*tu*' was a serious one, governed by surprisingly tight guiding rules (something once standard practice, now a matter of choice). Here Beckett judges that the apprenticeship is over: formality can move to intimacy. But what we read bypasses all contextualising. The change in relation is proposed in a phrase of Beckett's invention. There is no '*vous garou*', but there is a '*loup-garou*' (werewolf; the 'bogeyman' of children's stories and nursemaids' warnings). Beckett here banishes the bogeyman '*vous*'. So far so (relatively) easy. But how to render into English a shift (formal to informal) which has no direct or even approximate equivalent in modern usage? Two possibilities: record the expression as untranslatable, and write a note of the kind I have just given; or try to find an expression that does draw on English resources. My choice was the old Quaker refusal of conventional politenesses, which at least raises the issue. There is no matching Beckett's brevity, but an echo perhaps, both of the meaning and of Beckett's bold joke: 'Shall we stop the scraping and bowing, and go for thee-ing and thou-ing?'.

LETTING GO

In the mid-1970s, the *TLS* sent me for review Beckett's *Pour finir encore et autres foirades*: a small collection of short pieces. I read and reread the high-density texts, came to terms with these new utterances, contrived some sort of review, and dutifully posted it off. Time, quite a lot of time, passed. The (apprehensively) expected galley-proofs failed to appear. Then a small package was delivered, sent by a senior *TLS* figure. It contained a copy of *For to end yet again*, and a handwritten note. It appeared that, by some inexplicable confusion, my galleys had been dispatched to an American political historian. Now the senior figure wanted to know if this text was 'different from *Pour finir encore*'. If I could have answered that question, everything that needed to be known about Samuel Beckett would be known.

Send a few words on a
card addressed to this address:

4 Rue POUCHET
Paris 18ème

It is visited now many
by painters. It's about
what should be the end
of it. Entire contents
Pierre will have your hustled
and it's a mess too. I'm
so excited at a al last.

Rehearsals begin next
Monday. We had a
pleasant evening with
the Blins + Matias.

We are happy here
and aft... be missing
badly someone as much work.

Looking forward to
seeing you all soon &
we are great fans &
I'll give you up to..

Much love from us
both to you both.

152   16.

Pierre inquires about
viewing the all guarantee
Company, appears it be.
fares are too... it 10¢
will be in plenty of time.

Love to all, cincerrest
wishes, Eileen for

Feb. 15th.

I had read hardly more than a page of the English text before registering unease. I hurried past the passage which seemed to contain the immediate cause of this reaction, and, without any clear notion why, calmed down. That calm lasted until the next disturbing moment or passage, a page or two later. Something was the matter, but I was having great difficulty in formulating it. I made myself stare at it, speak it, then close my eyes and recite it, concerned only with its sounds and rhythm. 'They carry face to face and relay each other often so that turn about they backward lead the way. His who follows who knows to shape the course much as the coxswain with light touch the skiff.' This is his translation of 'Ils portent vis-à-vis et souvent se relaient si bien qu'à tour de rôle ils ouvrent la marche à reculons. A celui qui la ferme revient qui sait le soin de gouverner un peu comme par petites touches le barreur le skiff.' The word-ordering in the French makes the meaning immediately clear, with a distinctly Latinate flavour. But the English?

The syntax has gone beyond what English will allow. That perception prompted in me the still more unwelcome extension: Beckett's English is going, from that title on. Why the 'For'? It doesn't fit with modern English usage. It does fit with Irish usage – but not educated usage. This is rural Irish.

Over the next few months I worried intermittently about all this. I had no wish to talk to anyone about it. I had to fight my own battles, and could hardly bear to think about what was happening. Then, one day, the whole edifice of fear and doubt collapsed: undermined by the one person who could achieve this, Samuel Beckett. It was his latest published work, That Time, with its powerful evocation of a young man's world – and English word-world. Now I could even admit to what I had been fearing. And the fears had gone.

INTERNATIONAL LANGUAGE

Over the last century and a half a number of attempts have been made to invent and promote an 'international language': Esperanto, Interlingua, Interglossa, Ido... All were designed in the hope of overcoming the barriers created by foreignness, allowing

Riverdy dans le lieu indiqué. Le
résultat est pareil. que les ait
l'aient abattu ou qu'elles n'y a
pas encore tout à fait arrivé. c
sans importance. D'accord, puis
ne viens pas très bien, mais ce
moments c'est incomparable. a
aussi on nous tolle nos papillons
resteront toujours quelques chenilles.

        Je vous renouvelle mes vœux
vous, bon voyage et bon repos dans
fin d'après-midi, sauf contre-a
je dois maintenant ou attendre
         toilette de ma
qui s'appellerait probablement
attendant Godot. Je pour inten
vien dégager d'amis.

                  affectueusement

nation to reach out in peace to nation. All bear witness to a touchingly naive optimism; most have sunk virtually without trace in the public arena. The implicit claim is that they could eventually make translation irrelevant or unnecessary. They are devised by people, linguists usually, who are very well aware of the plurality and variety of languages, but whose awareness does not take into account those people who deliberately involve themselves with more than one natural (that is, living) language: those for whom it is not just mother tongue versus the rest. And the 'deliberately' needs qualification. Speakers of Hungarian, Swedish, even Dutch know that few foreigners will trouble to learn their language, and the pressures of commerce make it next to obligatory for them to learn at least one other language, usually now English. But this is different from the case of those who, without external pressures, immerse themselves in the study and practice of another language, or other languages. With the disappearance of Latin as a pan-European language, there is no short cut. The astonishing thing is that there are people who not only take up this learning with enthusiasm, who indeed rejoice in the gradual widening of their hold on more than one language, but create a supra-national situation in which they speak or write these languages in ways that suggest a new kind of pan-Europeanism: a recognition of each separate reality and its relation to other linguistic realities.

Beckett is the outstanding example of such a person. Starting, in childhood, from one language only (English), he gradually acquires, through study and experience, familiarity with French, Latin, Italian, German, and Spanish. Increasingly, his own expressiveness is affected by his recourse to these languages: they are optional directions in which he can invest himself, optional inflections of what he has to say. 'This vitaccia is terne beyond all belief,' he writes to Tom MacGreevy, combining Italian and French with his English. We cannot claim that Beckett was an English-language writer who also wrote in French (or the reverse): he is someone who wrote in English *and* wrote in French. Nor is this a matter only of self-translation, although he does a good deal of that. Some works are *conceived and written* in one language or the other, and may or may not be subsequently translated into the other.

Such assertions are likely to bring up the issue of formal compe-
tence. Beckett himself implicitly recognises this: his published
work is in English and French only. But with the letters we meet
something quite different – his recurrent scanning of his language-
range for the word or words that will best express what he wants to
say. This is no occasional or local matter: at any point – and at any
length: sentences, whole paragraphs – the text may move from
one language to another. It is, quite simply, his *natural* utterance:
something increasingly strange to the largely monoglot English.

PARATAXIS

Something at once odd and recurrent, an unpredictable switch
to understatement. Beckett's work in the Resistance has been
described in some detail; but never by him. The horrors of war
and Occupation are vividly present to him: he will not write
about them. What we know of his loyalty to his friends will tell
us what their death means to him; he will not. What we see is a
sort of crack in the surface of his writing; we have ourselves to
imagine what lies beneath it. Not far away is a related reticence:
the frequent inability or unwillingness of Holocaust survivors to
speak of their experience. Beckett talks, unforgettably, of the need
to express: but expressing is not turning on a confessional tap. In
the *locus classicus*, the letters to Duthuit, Beckett launches huge
sentences in which, as one clause succeeds or reverts to another,
he strives to convert hunch into judgement, reaching into the
ragbag of memory for examples and associations. These letters
are often about painting, and the letters themselves almost appear
as broad, even wild brushstrokes. But the headlong movement
always comes to an end, leaving the question of what comes
next. Sometimes, self-consciousness surges up, and there follows
a deflationary clause or sentence, rueful or embarrassed, as in the
sentence that follows an intensely-felt argument about the need
for lessness, renunciation: '*Mais je commence à écrire*' ('But I'm
beginning to *write*').

Immediately after giving (to his friend Tom MacGreevy) a
detailed account of the Irish Red Cross Hospital in Saint-Lô where

he worked as interpreter after the Allied landings in Normandy, Beckett writes: 'Robert Desnos (*Corps et biens*) died like Péron on his way home from deportation'. Desnos he knew slightly; Péron was a very close friend. There is no further comment.

How is it that anyone from Ireland will know immediately and exactly what the voice that Beckett describes sounded like, and what social stratum the speaker belonged to? (This particular voice belonged to Bobby Childers – as it happens, a member of a patrician Irish family – and is so described in a letter to Tom MacGreevy.) It's not as if all English voices sounded the same, or even that the Irish think they do. No need to rehearse in detail the unlovely story of the Englishing of Ireland: simply that the dominant figures (government, families, individuals) tended to speak in a particular, unforgettable way, in which even volume was a factor: these were people unafraid to take centre stage. The reaction of the locals ran from loathing to awe, by way of fear and forelock-touching, in recognition of difference and power. This was the vocal presence of the Master Race.

When, centuries ago, English rule came to Ireland, it soon became apparent to the new rulers that the language of the natives, since it was incomprehensible, was a danger: something round which this rebellious people could rally, in which they could with impunity conspire. It had to be proscribed: learn English or suffer the consequences. In the areas where the two groups overlapped, the policy worked: English eventually became the common language. Common nouns and verbs could be changed, but speech rhythms were a very different matter – and the Gaelic rhythms *were* very different. The word 'English' pointed to two realities, the scale of difference varying with person, education, occupation, circumstance. Not much had changed by the time the young Beckett became conscious of language-choices.

Mon cher vieux Georges

Assez de ce vous garoux, veux-tu?

Ta très belle lettre ce matin. Elle me
pour que je puisse me soucier de ma nage.
signaux, après lecture répétée. Je tâchera

Bram et moi, nous sommes loin l'un de l
devinés, quoique réunis à un moment, c'est
un même coincement, car il y en a qui ne l
non, pas de ça. C'est un endroit xxxxxx (
tout en termes de boîte) d'où l'on ne peut
paces que tu énumères, et certes Bram n'y
Mais il s'y essaie, ou y tient si tu préf
à mesure une espace paradis qui l'y autori
xxxxx traînent forcément quelques réminisc
ment mis à notre disposition et dont tant
ment gargarisés et dont d'autres encore on
fait leur affaire, comme il semble naturel
face contre mauvaise fortune, à supposer q
tous finissent bien par s'assoupir dans l'
Pardonne ce ton doctoral, mais sous le bon
aussi c'est un mauvais pas, d'où chaque fo
foudroiement - et ces longs silences où il
pour rien qu'il parle si souvent de domine
dire de sortir, et on voit de lui émerger
l'an dont il ne veut pas, une main, une ép
vers la prise qu'il n'a pas su s'assurer.
qu'il finirait par y renoncer, par peindre
que par épuisement. Il m'a semblé voir s'
dans certaines toiles, par exemple dans la
et d'une façon beaucoup plus nette et dram
unes des grandes gouaches sombres exposées
absolument que tu ailles voir chez Boré. M
depuis quelque temps qu'il est trop tard e
fin ces formidables tentatives de rétablis
furieusement rêvée, et qu'à vrai dire il p
ce sera chez lui jusqu'à la fin la seule b
l'échec, au lieu de celle, tellement calme
la prétention de me laisser hanter. N'empê
une peinture sans précédent et où je trouv
nulle autre, à cause justement de cette fi
de ce refus d'une liberté à surveiller. De
il se trouve de reconnaître à son trou, to
xxxxxxxxxxxxxx s'y arracher, la liberté,

e plonge dans trop de courants
. Donc séulement quelques
rai qu'ils soient simples.

e l'autre, si je nous ai bien
st à dire à tout moment, dans
lâchent pas. Je veux dire -
(drôle que je voie toujours
ut sortir vers aucun des es-
y parvient pas plus que moi.
fères, en se creant au fur et
rise, espace nouveau où
scences de ceux si génereuse-
t d'artistes se sont si belle-
ont simplement pris leur parti,
rel en effet qu'on fasse bonne
qu'elle soit mauvaise, et
l'unanimité faite à ce sujet.
onnet quel chahut. Pour Bram
fois ces montagnes et ce
il récupère. Ce n'est pas
iner et de vaincre, c'est à
er en effet, 5 ou 6 fois par
épaule, on oeil, implorant
. J'ai cru à un moment donné
re le coincement, ne serait-ce
s'amorcer cette grande aventure
la peinture qui est chez toi,
ramatique encore dans quelques-
ées chez Michaud et qu'il faut
. Mais je commence à croire
et que ce sera jusqu'à la
lissement vers une cime
porte dans ses bras, et que
beauté de l'effort et de
me et même gaie, dont j'ai
pêche que pour moi ça reste
uve mon compte comme dans
fidélité à l'oubliette et
De cette nécessité de génie où
tout en s'obstinant à vouloir
des xxxxx hauteurs, la lumière

Beckett writes to Duthuit of the need to strip away all vanity, all aspiration. He calls for *'le débarras d'au moins une bonne partie de ce que nous avons cru avoir de meilleur, ou de plus réel, au prix de quels efforts, et peut-être l'immense simplicité d'une partie au moins du peu redouté que nous sommes et avons'*. The opening allows some sense of the general direction: 'the shedding of at least a good part of what we thought we had that was best, or most real, at the cost of what efforts. And perhaps the immense simplicity of part at least of the' – followed by the impenetrably dense or refined 'peu redouté que nous sommes et avons'. I stayed with the outline of these words and wrote: 'of the little feared that we are and have'. At best I can offer a tentative paraphrase: 'We are hardly at all redoubtable, and possess nothing that could be called redoubtable', and suppose that this too is to be shed – in spite of its 'immense simplicity'.

Beckett's profound admiration for the painting of Bram van Velde issues in a language of exceptional complexity, but seldom on the scale he manages in a letter to Duthuit of March 1949: *'Et*

ces splendeurs où j'entends l'hymne de l'être fonçant à rebours et libre enfin dans les quartiers interdits, ce sont peut-être des splendeurs comme tant d'autres, rapport à l'espèce bien sûr, celle de la corde tendue où l'on se vautre'. 'And these splendours', he writes, 'in which I can hear the hymn of Being blasting out back to front, and free at last in the forbidden quarters, are perhaps splendours like so many others, *rapport à l'espèce* of course, that of the tightrope that we sprawl over'. The words I have italicised mean, literally, 'in relation to', and 'species or kind'. English speakers occasionally use 'species' as a shorthand for 'human species', but the French do not. I settle (uneasily) for 'species', which is difficult and puzzling, rather than 'kind' or 'sort' which I judge impossible ('thinking of the kind, that of...'?; 'in relation to the sort, that of'?). Beckett is qualifying his admiration, while holding out against the qualification ('it suits me better not to believe it'). I am not clear what he is in fact proposing... *Mais je commence à désespérer* – But I'm beginning to despair.

Thus Beckett to Duthuit when, in 1949, he finds himself totally unable to write the commentary on Bram van Velde that Duthuit has asked of him, wondering if the reason might not be his having to write it directly in English, this 'horrible langue' which he still knows too well. Why 'horrible', rather than 'misérable' or 'lamentable', or some other indicator of calm distancing?

It is perilously easy to see Beckett's move to French as the outcome of a datable decision, when what is at issue is closer to an existential reorientation which began in the 'lost' years spent in hiding in Unoccupied France, during which Beckett is exposed to an undifferentiated tide of French – no longer only the currency of artists and intellectuals, but the language of farm, forge, garage, and inn. The thought that he could now 'take on' that language for his own creative purposes grows in force, and, as the end of the War signals a universal reconstruction, the chance comes to act on it. It is a huge risk, but he takes it, and, in order to take it, he pushes English away. But of course English is not so easily repudiated, and has a lifetime's coils wrapped round him. Revealingly, of the horrible language he says, *'que je sais trop bien'*, using the verb *'savoir'* rather than *'connaître'*, suggesting as it does embedded knowledge rather than mere familiarity. A time will come when he can think more steadily about English. That time was not the summer of 1949.

CHANGING HORSES (3)

In a letter to Duthuit, Beckett, gloomily aware of diminished physical powers, says *'je sens que l'heure de ma retraite sans flambeaux, je me demande de quoi, est proche'*. Starting with the phrase *'retraite aux flambeaux'* (solemn torchlit procession), which he immediately and typically downgrades (no torches, but keeping the element of retreat), he restores the solemnity with *'proche'*. We have no social equivalent to the *'retraite aux flambeaux'*, so I concentrate on that side of it that depends on formal organisation and try 'my unceremonial retreat, from what, I wonder, is nigh'. That last word worries me: it is solemn all right, too solemn for

Samuel Beckett. Thinking it over further, I might wish to change 'is nigh' to 'is upon me'.

Duthuit is familiar with Beckett's delight in the non-decorative aspect of gardening: digging, mowing, planting. Beckett brings him up to date in the same letter, informing his friend, '*Je mange déjà, tiens-toi bien, mes propres oignons, c'est bien la première fois que je m'en découvre*'. I try 'I am already, do not miss this, eating my own onions. It is the first time that I . . . ', before being overtaken by a problem. The sentence is clearly about the sudden and pleasurable realisation of ownership, possession; but the expression is awkward (the French construction too is slightly odd, and could not have been predicted). The most direct rendering would be 'find myself having any', but that seems clumsy. Can it be made less so? I try the more elaborate: 'I've ever found myself in a position to have any'. Not just more elaborate: laborious. Is there a neater rendering? I have not yet found one. The struggle goes on – *la chasse continue*.

Affectueusement

BECKETT: THE PROBLEM (BECKETT: THE SOLUTION)

Why did Beckett move to writing in French? It would be (relatively) easy to tell the story in straight, or straight-ish, biographical terms: events, dates, declared reasons, external pressures, general context, decisions. But only people who know little or nothing about language(s) could imagine that a writer who was not bilingual from his infancy would simply *decide* to write in another language: as it might be, turn on this tap rather than that. He or she might indeed formulate the decision (we all need to believe that we can break with habit), but the thought would be followed immediately by profound anxieties: if the writing is to be published, how will its readers react? Can I hold my nerve as I hear the scornful laughter of the native speakers? Only the supremely confident could meet that challenge without flinching (a Nabokov, perhaps). But what of the writer who does not have an ironclad temperament?

In Beckett's case, unlike that of Nabokov, there are no external political realities constraining his choices; he can go on being an English-language writer as long as he wishes. His education, his experience of France and the French, and, underlying all this, his profound openness to the word in all its forms, in any of the languages he has engaged with – these make the possibility of the switch a potentially achievable reality. That is where the *work* begins: the actual forging of text in the other language. For Beckett the linguist there remained the intensities, pleasures, worries, hopes and acceptances that went with investment in the new language; but, more important even than these, the unspeakable joy of deploying the self, day in, day out, in these 'alien' words.

Could he himself have told us all that, in simple words?

Je t'en fous. Could he hell. (?)

What stays always with me as translator is the sound of Beckett's voice; something that he *does* find simple words to represent: '*seule la voix est, bruissant et laissant des traces*', words which he translates as 'there is nothing but a voice murmuring a trace'.

I for once would argue with him, and let his words say: 'only the voice *is,* making faint sounds and leaving traces'.

What traces.

Notes

p. 8   Letter to GD, 12 August 1948.

p. 11A   Letter to Tom MacGreevy, 23 April 1933.

p. 11B   Letter to GD, 1 March 1949.

p. 12A   T. S. Eliot, 'East Coker', from *The Four Quartets*.

p. 12B   Letter to GD, 1 March 1949.

p. 12C   Letter to GD, 27 February 1950.

p. 13   Letter to GD, on or after 30 April, before 26 May 1949.

p. 16   Letter to Georges Duthuit, 10 March 1949

p. 17   Letter to GD, 2 August 1948.

p. 22A   'What is the Word.'

p. 22B   Letter to Mania Péron, 17 August 1951.

p. 22C   Letter to GD, 11 August 1948.

p. 22D   Letter to Jérôme Lindon, 20 January 1954.

p. 24   Letter to GD, 2 March 1949.

p. 28   Letter to Tom MacGreevy, 24 February 1931.

p. 29   Letter to GD, 11 August 1948.

p. 30A   Letter to Tom MacGreevy, 19 January 1945.

p. 30B   Letter to Tom MacGreevy, 25 March 1936.

p. 33   Letter to GD, 11 August 1948.

p. 34A   Letter to GD, undated (28 June 1949?).

p. 34B   Letter to GD, 9-14 April 1941.

p. 36   *Textes pour rien / Texts for Nothing*, XIII.

Images

FRONTISPIECE: clockwise from top: stamp on envelope to Avigdor Arikha; picture postcard of Le Lapin Agile, Montmartre, to AA, 28 August 1986; picture postcard of Val Ferret, Courmayeur, to AA, 16 July 1966; picture postcard of Nazaré, Portugal, to AA, 6 January 1970; picture postcard of Courmayeur, to AA, 28 August 1966; p. 7, card to Claude Duthuit (Georges Duthuit's son); p. 10, SB to GD, 20 July 1951; p. 15, SB to GD, undated (before 23 September 1949); pp. 18-19, SB to GD, undated (1949?); p. 25, SB to Edward Beckett, 21 august 1963; p. 27, SB to GD, undated (March 1949?); pp. 31-32, SB to GD, 2 March 1949; p. 33, SB signature on undated card to AA; p. 35, SB signature on undated letter to GD (March 1950?); p. 39, top, stamp on envelope to Edward Beckett.

COLOPHON

THE CAHIERS SERIES · NUMBER 16
ISBN: 978-0-9565092-7-7

Printed by Principal Colour, Paddock Wood, on
Neptune Unique (text) and Chagall (dust jacket).
Set in Giovanni Mardersteig's Monotype Dante.

With grateful thanks to the Florence Gould
Foundation for its support.

Series Editor: Dan Gunn
Design: Ornan Rotem

CENTER FOR WRITERS & TRANSLATORS
THE AMERICAN UNIVERSITY OF PARIS

SYLPH EDITIONS, LONDON | 2011

THE AMERICAN
UNIVERSITY
OF PARIS

center for writers and translators

SYLPH
EDITIONS

www.aup.fr · www.sylpheditions.com